Ghost Docs on Patrol

Collins
YELLOW
Storybook

Other Collins Yellow Storybooks

Ghost Docs on Patrol

SCOULAR ANDERSON

CollinsChildren'sBooks
An imprint of HarperCollins*Publishers*

First published in Great Britain by CollinsChildren'sBooks 1998

1 3 5 7 9 11 11 10 8 6 4 2

CollinsChildren'sBooks is a division of
HarperCollins*Publishers* Ltd,
77-85 Fulham Palace Road,
Hammersmith, London W6 8JB

The HarperCollins website address is
www.**fire**and**water**.com

Text and illustrations copyright © Scouler Anderson 1998

ISBN 0 00 765348 4

Printed and bound in Great Britain by
Bookmarque Ltd, Croydon, Surrey

It was midnight.

Nocto, the ghost, switched off his alarm

and floated out of his hammock.

He put on his
floppy green hat
and was ready
for the night's
work.

Then another alarm went off. It
was Nocto's Ghostfax, but Nocto
could not remember where he had
put it. He was always losing things.

He tried all the pockets of his
ghostsuit.

He tried his side pockets.

Then he tried his
back pockets...
and his top
pockets.

He even tried
under his hat!

At last he found it.

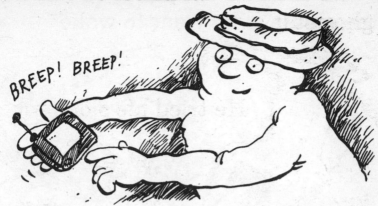

BREEP! BREEP!

He switched on the Ghostfax. It began to print a message.

EMERGENCY!!
GHOST DOCS WANTED
AT 4.

There was a haunt breakdown at 45 Fishyfin Street. Mrs Arabella Frightly needed the Ghost Docs.

When Nocto had finished reading
the message he went to wake
Squibbly.

But Squibbly didn't want to get up.
He wanted five more minutes to
snooze!

There was only one thing to do.

Nocto tipped Squibbly out of his hammock.

"Come on Squibbly," he said. "This is an emergency. We have to go to 45 Fishyfin Street quickly. Mrs Arabella Frightly has reported a haunt breakdown."

Nocto sent Squibby to fetch the Bag of Tricks. "Bring anything we might need from the medicine cupboard, too," he said.

Nocto started the scooter and the Ghost Docs were ready for action.

CHAPTER

As they sped through the air on their scooter Nocto sang the Ghost Docs' song:

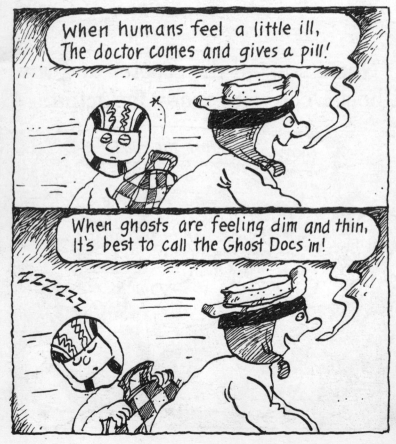

When humans feel a little ill,
The doctor comes and gives a pill!

When ghosts are feeling dim and thin,
It's best to call the Ghost Docs in!

ZZZZZZ

Nocto took a short cut down a lane.
They passed some cats sitting on
dustbins.

Squibbly wanted to practise his
haunting.

He pulled a face at the cats. It was
his scariest face.

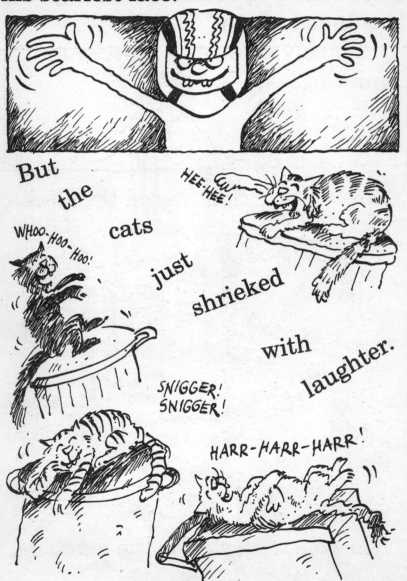

But the cats just shrieked with laughter.

HEE-HEE!

WHOO-HOO-HOO!

SNIGGER!
SNIGGER!

HARR-HARR-HARR!

Nocto was cross. "That's not the way to do it," he said. "I'll show you how to scare cats."

Nocto drove right round the block.

The cats were still on the dustbins.

Nocto drove straight *at* the dustbins. "YAAAAARRRROOOOO!" he screamed.

The cats were terrified. Nocto gave them a *real* scare! The cats ran for their lives. The bins fell over, the lids fell off, the rubbish fell out. There was a terrible noise.

CLANG!

THUMP!

BLUMP!

BEEOING

RATTLE!

"That's the way to do it, Squibbly," said Nocto. "That's the way to make humans jump in their beds, too!"

Nocto revved up the scooter and off they sped.

VROOOOM!

At last Nocto and Squibbly arrived
at 45 Fishyfin Street.

It was very quiet.

It was much *too* quiet!

There was no noise at all.

There was no sign
of a haunting.

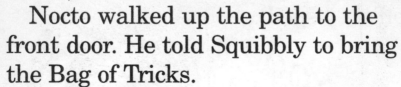

Nocto walked up the path to the
front door. He told Squibbly to bring
the Bag of Tricks.

Nocto drew a deep breath and made himself very thin.

Then he slipped... and slithered...

and slid through the letterbox.

He landed gently on the hall floor.

Now it was Squibbly's turn. But Squibbly didn't slip. He didn't slither. Squibbly... got stuck!

Nocto began to pull Squibbly. He pulled... and pulled... and pulled.

Squibbly and the Bag of Tricks
landed on the hall floor... with a
bump!

Nocto looked around the hall. "Hello," he called. "Any ghost at home?"

There was no reply.

Nocto decided to make some notes, but he could not remember where he had put his notebook. He tried all his pockets... again.

When he had found his notebook, he set off through the house to make notes.

He popped his head into the
sitting room.

He looked into the cupboard under
the stairs

He slithered into the dining room.

He opened the back door.
There was no noise anywhere.

He went into the kitchen. There was a funny noise in there.

It was the cat... snoring.

Then he went upstairs to look in the bedrooms.

There were funny noises in the big bedroom. More snoring.

He was just going into the small bedroom when... he felt a haunting in the air.

Mr and Mrs Frightly had appeared. They were the ghosts who had just moved into 45 Fishyfin Street, but they were not happy. There was something wrong with their new house.

"It doesn't have that haunted feeling," said Arabella Frightly.

"What are *you* going to do about it?" she asked Nocto.

Nocto looked for his notebook again.

He searched in all his pockets until he found it.

He showed Mr and Mrs Frightly what he had written.

ROOM1 - Silence
ROOM2 - Silence
ROOM3 - Silence
ROOM4 - SNORING!
ROOM5 - SNORING!

Then he jumped up and down on the spot. "Listen. Not a squeak," he said.

He opened a door. "Listen. Not a creak," he said.

Then he opened a cupboard door. "Not a squeak and not a creak! There is too much silence and too much...

SNORING... SQUIBBLY!"

Squibbly was asleep in the
cupboard. Nocto pulled him out.

"Squeaking floors and creaking doors, stop peaceful sleep and heavy snores!" Nocto said to Mrs Frightly. "If you want this house to feel a bit more *haunted*, you want a bit more *creaking* and a bit more *squeaking*."

Nocto began to search in his pockets – again!

At last he found what he was looking for.

He held up a small thing like a grain of rice.

The thing was small,
but it was very noisy.
Nocto squeezed it
a few times.

CREEAK! CREEEAK! CREEEAK!

It was a
special Ghost
Doc Creaker
to make a quiet house nice and noisy.

Mrs Frightly did *not* look pleased.
"How will that silly thing make my
house noisy?" she said.

SQUEEEAK! CREEEAK!

Stuff and nonsense!

We've been listening to you chatter on for quite long enough!

We haven't time to float around here all night...

...and we don't trust that sleepy helper of yours.

These young ghostkids want to spend all night in their hammocks!

Nocto tried to explain what he
was going to do with the Creaker,

but he could not get a word in
edgeways.

Nocto knew he would have to take drastic action. He clicked his fingers. "Squibbly, bring the Bag of Tricks," he said.

"And get out the Ghostvax."

Nocto switched on the Ghostvax and sucked Mr and Mrs Frightly into it.

Then he put the lid on the Ghostvax. "Right, Squibbly, let's get to work," he said.

Nocto had a plan. He would put Creakers under every floorboard and Squeakers behind every door.

Squiggly rummaged in the Bag of
Tricks and found a whole bag of
Creakers and a whole bag of
Squeakers.

"Good," said Nocto. "We'll soon
have this house creaking like an old
ship – a ghost ship! That will make
Mrs Frightly feel much better."

Nocto looked around the hall.
There were things all over the carpet.
He would have to clear them up to
get to the floorboards.

Nocto bossed Squibbly around and Squibbly did all the hard work.

Backwards and forwards he went...

and up and down...

...until the hall was cleared. Then he rolled up the carpet.

Now Nocto started searching in his pockets again!

He pulled out a screwdriver and started to unscrew some floorboards.

Squibbly brought the bag of Creakers, but just as they started to put them under the floorboards there was a noise from upstairs. A strange wailing sort of noise.

It went something like, "*Daaaad. Daaaaad. I wanna drink of water.*"

Then there was another noise – the sound of footsteps.

Squibbly quickly rolled the carpet back over the floor.

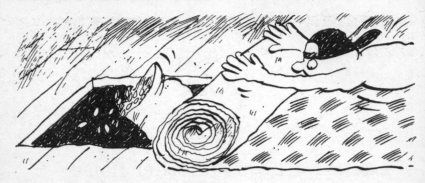

He was just in time.

A man walked across the hall to the kitchen.

The carpet sagged into the hole in the floor. Then he walked back again with a glass of water in his hand.

When the man had gone upstairs, Nocto said, "Phew! That was close. We had better finish this job quickly."

Nocto rolled up the carpet again.
He gave the roll a good kick.

But he could not
see the bags of
Creakers and
Squeakers.

Squibbly
had gone,
too.

Nocto heard a noise coming from under the floorboards. He peered into the hole.

There were mice everywhere. Then there was a noise from upstairs again. *"Daaad, Daaad, I wanna biscuit!"*

Nocto hid.

The man came down into the hall in his bare feet.

He reached for the table lamp. But there was no lamp, no table and no carpet.

Just then, Squibbly tried to slither out of the rolled carpet. His ghostly hand appeared.

"Help," cried the man, when he saw Nocto's head. "We are being haunted."

He ran upstairs to the big bedroom. He needed to get help.

By the time he came back downstairs, Nocto and Squibbly had put everything back.

"That was a good night's work," said Nocto.

"But, we didn't get the Creakers *under* the floorboards," said Squiggly. "Or the Squeakers behind the doors. The mice ate them all!"

"That's right," said Nocto, "so now we have mobile Squeakers and Creakers. The house will never be quiet again. There will be no more haunt breakdowns at 45 Fishyfin Street."

Creeeak!
squeak!
Creeeak!

Squeak!
Squeeeak!
Squeal!

Nocto picked up the Ghostvax and took the lid off. Mr and Mrs Frightly came floating out. "What happened?" cried Arabella Frightly.

"You have just had a little rest, Madam," said Nocto. "Now, please listen."

Mrs Frightly listened, then smiled. "Ah, that's better!" she said. A house feels more haunted when it's filled with creaks and squeaks!"

"And when humans are too scared to sleep," said Nocto.

Squibbly floated off to the kitchen to find something to eat. He was wide awake now and he was starving.

But there was something in the kitchen.

It was a girl, in a horrible dog mask.

Squibbly tried to look as scary as possible. But he wasn't very good at scaring.

The girl in the kitchen started to laugh. She said to Squibbly, "Stop being silly and get me a biscuit please. I can't reach the tin."

"OK," said Squibbly, "but we need to do a swap."

Nocto and Squibbly were ready to go home.

"Load the Bag of Tricks, Squibbly," said Nocto. "We'll drive past the cats in the lane again. You could do with some scaring practice!"

It had been a good night's work for Squibbly too. He scared the cats till they ran away!